VELAZQUEZ

by
José Manuel Pita Andrade

photography
Eleonor Domínguez Ramírez

MADRID
1 9 7 6

Translated by:
Patricia S. Parrent

Original Title:
Velázquez Pintor Esencial
I. S. B. N.: 84-85041-14-3

© 1976 by SILEX
Cid, 4 - N.º 502 - Madrid-1

I. S. B. N.: 84-85041-03-8
Copyright: M. 18.702-1976

© 1972 by Eleonor Domínguez. Madrid

Printed in Spain by
Grafiplás, S. A. - Aranjuez, 7 - Madrid-20

(Printed in Spain)

CONTENTS

Paint, really paint?
No one ever did it better.

SINGULARITY AND UNIVERSALITY

The words of Eugenio D'Ors about *The Weavers* which head this chapter (1) fully define Velázquez's meaning for the history of art. His name must always be recalled in conjunction with the world of painting on an essential level. All those who aid in ranking the figure of this extraordinary person in history must subordinate themselves to this supreme value. And it is perhaps due to a mandate of history that, in order to affirm this superior ranking, the most important things we know about Velázquez we know through his paintings. Because the contemporary texts and documents almost always leave us unsatisfied with their administrative dryness —when they are not disconcerting. There are very few documents by the artist's hand and they do not help to understand his inner world. According to comments by Philip IV, we know that he had an easy-going character, which must have helped him overcome some difficult moments. Outside of this, everything is guesswork. And since there is much we do not know about his personality, it was inevitable that people would try to uncover it by means of guesses which oft-times went too far afield.

Now that the celebration of the tercentenary of his death begins to be left behind, our view of Velázquez has begun to become clear thanks not only to tireless investigation in the archives or the critical analyses of his works, but also thanks to wise interpretations by people who are not art scholars. We should think of the penetrating opinions of a philosopher like Ortega y Gasset (2) and the theses of a historian like Maravall (3) or of a dramatist like Buero Vallejo (4); nor may the testimony of the poets (5) be forgotten.

The present moment now permits a broader view of Velázquez's figure, something which could not be affirmed only a few decades ago. And, nevertheless, his true worth is poorly understood by many of the visitors to the Prado Museum. Everyone stops with pleasure in front of his most famous canvases. You don't have to have an especially trained eye to enjoy contemplating *The Lances, The Weavers, The Maids of Honor* or *The Court Jesters*. Velázquez's language is apparently simple; and for this reason the spectator is soon satisfied and does not feel the need to ask anything about the picture. As if the artist were telling us everything which needed to be said by means of the brush strokes which hold up a "photographic" representation of reality. In this seeming facility of expression the greatest risk is found. Besides seeing Velázquez's work, we must understand it. And to do this it is necessary to enter into a series of problems which acquire unexpected dimensions and often remain unsolved. When these questions are broached, the two perspectives which serve as the title for this chapter appear and they require a previous analysis.

To call Velázquez a singular artist may seem too elemental. His genius has always been uncontested. But the understanding of his work requires that he be seen not only in conjunction with his own times (which were those of Descartes), but also as distinguished from the contemporary Spanish painters who could and must have been his friends, Zurbarán or Alonso Cano, for example. Isolated in solitude, even separated from the Court, Velázquez's world is that of a continual experimentation with the problems which affect painting without renouncing the fertile stimulus of the works of other great masters which surrounded him in the old Alcázar in Madrid. Alone, and at a measured pace, Velázquez went along creating a style which set him apart from the other painters. For this reason, it is difficult to place him in the Sevillian school, is spite of having been born in Seville, or in the Madrilenian one, in spite of his years of residence at Court. Thus an extremely paradoxical fact results: although he is the most important Spanish painter of the 17th century, he does not serve to characterize the Spanish painting of his times. His painting is so much his own that it has not even been carried on by a wide circle of students and imitators, as happened with Rubens. Next to Velázquez, Velázquian style is rather limited. But think, in contrast, what the school of the Master from Antwerp signified.

The singularity of Velázquez is conditioned by his own mode life and by a series of circumstances which set him apart from the life styles of the other painters. From the moment he establishes himself at the Court and fills a series of positions there, he no longer paints for a living and perhaps that is why he worked calmly. Finding himself inside the Alcázar with a fabulous collection of pictures by other masters (we should not forget the extremely first-rate works by the great Venetian masters, still represented better in the Prado Museum today than in any other museum in the world) and knowing Rubens personally, he had the good fortune to form his artistic taste inside Spain in conditions not available to the normal painters. Besides, a great part of the pictures which he was doing remained in the royal palaces as faithful witnesses to this own artistic development. This may explain the retouching or "repentances" which can be discovered in many canvases. Several years after they were finished they could be enriched with new brush strokes; thus the artist managed to modernize their style.

This painter who works without hurrying, who broadens the meaning of his art thanks to the constant study of the art works which surround him, who retouches his canvases and has close at hand the majority of his work, who leaves some paintings unfinished, poses serious problems for the critics of our times. Perhaps these singular circumstances explain why he painted so little. For rigorous critics the catalog of his works does not reach a hundred and fifty, although there exist notable fluctuations above and below this number (6). Nevertheless, the quality more than makes up for this and always serves as a standard for deciding upon the authenticity of the works. It could be that the superior level of his work is what caused the scarce diffusion of his style in other artists which was mentioned before. He did not leave much of a mark in the so-called Madrilenian school, but rather remained marvelously alone and above all the artists of the 17th century. Pareja, his servant and also a painter, scarcely shows any stylistic ties with his master. To the style of Velázquez adheres only his aid and son-in-law Juan Bautista Mazo, whose works are estimable when they are done in intimate contact with our master.

The notes of singularity are expressed above all when

remarking the quality of Velázquez's painting. But his exceptional place is also noted when comparing the pictorial genres he cultivated with those of the other artists. If in 17th-century Spanish painting there is a stifling predominance of religious themes, in Velázquez they are extremely scarce, especially after he leaves Seville. No Spaniard in his times cultivated the portrait genre as intensely, even if for obvious reasons. The mythological themes, practically excluded from Spanish Baroque painting, have a transcendental significance in Velázquez. His feeling for landscape also brings him to be set apart from other painters. Finally, still-lifes and historical paintings reached with this painter a true singularity.

Isolated from the Spanish painting of his times, it is not enough to place Velázquez on a different plane at a national level. In the measure in which he was sensitive to the most diverse stimuli (without forgetting that among them were those of his own country, such as in the case of El Greco), he stands as an artist who attempts to universalize the problems of painting. Draftsmanship, composition, color, the expression of space and light are questions which affect an art which does not recognize national borders, and after the intensive experimentation of the Renaissance, they had to crystalize in the Baroque style. Probably no other artist presents us with a more balanced assimilation of all these factors.

HIS LIFE AND WORK

Destiny seems to have wanted to distribute Velázquez's existence in a clear and harmonius trajectory. No great upsets or anxieties show up in his biography, at least in that part which may be traced with the aid of the texts and documents that have reached us. It is true that these testimonies do not allow us to delve into the most intimate parts of his life, but since he was spared facing poverty and serious family problems we may relate Velázquez's well-known phlegmatic character to the serene trajectory of his life. The dates also help to place him easily in the first six decades of the 17th century in a series of periods which have the property of being reflected in the painter's style.

Betwixt Light and Shadows: Seville (1599-1622)

As the 16th century ends, Diego de Silva is born in the lovely city on the Guadalquivir, joining the Portuguese blood of his father with his mother's Spanish blood. It is not very important to remember the family surroundings which place us in what we would today consider a middle-class home and in a richly stimulating atmosphere. Because Seville opens the 17th century as one of the major Spanish cities which has, besides, the privilege of being the bridgehead for America. It is the metropolis which is masterfully portrayed in Cervantes' *Rinconete and Cortadillo,* where the rogues roost alongside the cathedral; but there also exists a rich cultural background which manifests itself as much in the field of literature as in that of the plastic arts. Our great painter will benefit from all of this, and after an unsuccessful attempt at finding a teacher in Herrera, the Elder, he will happily discover in Francisco Pacheco (a good theoretician of art and mediocre painter) the excellent mentor he needed. In Pacheco's home he found the encouragement necessary to become known and triumph quickly; there he also resolved the sentimental question by marrying his teacher's daughter Juana at the age of eighteen.

As Velázquez studies in Pacheco's workshop he inmediately displays an extraordinary talent for draftsmanship and a drive to transfer the world which surrounds him to the canvas in a direct manner. Pacheco tells us that when he was a boy he had hired "a little country apprentice who served as a model, in diverse attitudes and postures, sometimes crying, other times laughing, without sparing him in the least" (7). Along with this preoccupation with direct study which is in accordance with the realistic sentiment which predominates in Spanish painting, there may be found and obsession with light which links Velázquez to the entire Tenebrist movement. Harsh, violent backlighting is manifested in a vigorous chiaroscuro which leaves little room for a show of color. Along this path he departs from the precepts defended by his teacher (who is more linked to the Renaissance ideals than to the Baroque innovations), but he adopts Caravaggio's style, which begins to be discovered in Seville at a decisive moment for Spanish painting, since along with Velázquez his contemporaries, Zurbarán and Alonso Cano, will also follow these new trends.

The Naturalist tendencies gel in Velázquez's youthful works in a series of pictures which are divided among collections which, in the main, are found outside of Spain. The majority may be classified as bodegones, although in the ways they are interpreted we may discover novelties which are worth taking into account. With vigorous contrasts of light, Velázquez manages to vitalize a genre which is also known by the name of "still-life". Along with some ceramic dishes, with a mortar, a basket, some fish or a few eggs, there is a human figure to liven up the scene. Thus there appear *The Musicians* in the Berlin Museum, *The Water Carrier* in the Wellington Collection, *The Old Woman Frying Eggs* in the Edinburgh Museum...; sometimes the scene in the foreground is complemented with a religious motif (*Christ in the House of Mary and Martha* in the National Gallery in London), which we don't know if is seen in a picture hanging on the wall or is reflected in a mirror. Pacheco tells us that the still-lifes "if they are painted as my son-in-law paints them... are worthy of the greatest esteem", since in them and in the portraits "he found the true imitation of nature" (8). Profoundly enchanting, these youthful works manifest great personality and a creative feeling, but they are only the point of departure as the fruit of transcendental youthful experiments.

Along with the bodegones, the portraits from the Sevillian period signify the point of departure for a genre which will constitute one of the most important goals in Velázquez's art. In Seville he captures the Andalusian types with strong physiognomical features which allow him to fix those of that "little country boy" whom Pacheco spoke of (could he be the one we see in *The Old Woman Frying Eggs* and in *The Water Carrier*?) and of the gypsies who maraud at the steps of the cathedral. Doing portraits Velázquez develops themes of an exclusively religious character: in *The Adoration of the Magi,* in the Prado Museum, the monarch closest to the Virgin is doubtlessly a gypsy type; Mary is probably Juana Pacheco, probably evoked once more in the *Immaculate Conception* in the Frere Collection in London.

Along with these personages which appear in the still-lifes or in the religious paintings we would also have to cite others which mark the beginning of his activity as a portrait artist in the strict sense. This is the case of *Don Cristóbal Suárez de la Ribera* (a canvas in the Seville Museum) or of *Sor Jerónima de la Fuente*, whose likeness survives in two almost identical versions (the Prado Museum and the Viuda de Araoz's Coll.) in which is compacted all the energy of the character of the old nun who embarked in Seville in 1520 to found a convent in the Philippines. The *Head of a Woman* which is reproduced in two drawings in the National Library makes us think of his wife. As the wrap up of his activity in Seville or the starting point for his following period, we will mention various portraits. In those of *Don Luis de Góngora,* known in two versions (in the Lázaro Galdiano Museum in Madrid and one in the Boston Museum; this last one had a crown of laurels which was later painted out), the great Baroque poet is masterfully captured. A personage with a ruffled collar, in the Prado Museum, perhaps offers us the first *Self-portrait.* Finally we must keep in mind the profile of a woman's head which makes us think once more of Juana Pacheco.

The Discovery of Venice in Madrid (1623-1628)

In 1622, Velázquez makes his first trip to Madrid. He is there several months during which he probably prepares his definitive establishment in the Court. There he is installed as the Painter to the King in October of 1623. This change of scene (as Ortega y Gasset so rightly observed) is the most important event in Velázquez's life. From then on his livelihood is taken care of, although more than once his activity will have to be spread to cover tasks alien to the art of painting. As time goes on, he will hold various positions (Usher of the King's Privy Chamber from 1627 to 1634, Valet of the King's Wardrobe from 1636, Valet of the King's Privy Chamber from 1634 and Palace Chamberlain from 1652) which occupy his time. Except for some moments of economic distress, he gets along without serious problems and also without living in luxury. But the most decisive thing is not that his life is resolved. It is the possibility of having around him an extremely rich collection of paintings. From the first moment he must have been attracted to the Venetians. If we think of the quality of the canvases by Titian, Veronese and Tintoretto which surrounded him we can realize that his discovery of Venice took place years before he was able to visit the City of the Canals.

In Madrid, Velázquez received great acclaim at once. He not only won over the King and the protection of the, at the time, all-powerful Count-Duke of Olivares, but he was also a success in the streets. The equestrian portrait of the King which was exhibited to the public on the steps of the no longer extant San Felipe el Real Convent, alongside the Calle Mayor, was famous. The canvas, unfortunately, has been lost (although perhaps a bust of *Philip IV* which is preserved in the Prado may be a fragment from it), was extremely lauded in great poems. The disappearance of this painting is compensated for by others of the sovereign, of his brother the *Infante Don Carlos,* and of the *Count-Duke of Olivares* which are characterized by the fact that these personages are shown standing, in an interior setting, dressed in black, with an intonation which already indicates fundamental changes in the vision of color and light. The brushwork has become less harsh; the earlier toasted colors are now substituted with gray tones and a noble bearing and severity predominates in the figures which match the atmosphere at the Court of the Austrias. The new elements which may be observed in the manner of placing the figures are interesting in spite of the retouching which may sometimes be discovered (the portrait of *Philip IV*), showing us the artist's vacilations.

Ortega says that "after his triumph in Madrid... the most important event in Velázquez's entire life is the visit which Rubens, at the height of his fame, made to Madrid in 1628-29" (9). Although this judgement might be a bit exaggerated, it is indubitable that the direct contact with Rubens had to have left a profound mark not only upon the painter, but also upon the man. Velázquez began to make his way in a complex Court which was still quite far from esteeming artists to the degree that the painter from Antwerp was in Flanders. The stay of Rubens (who came on a diplomatic mission) must have motivated Velázquez to enter into themes which he not handled before, such as mythological ones, and to visit Italy, with the King's help.

The first Madrilenian period closes with a work which merits special attention. By entering the world of myths Velázquez breaks with a norm of Spanish painting (in which this type of theme is so scarce), although he expresses them in a language different from that of the Italian or Flemish artists. This observation is important if we consider that there was no lack of examples for our artist to follow. From the very first, mythology is captured with a realistic feeling and perhaps with a subtle irony. The first picture in the series, *The Drinkers,* still possesses Tenebrist echoes. In it, several drinkers who are a bit high and who decide to make fun of the gods are grouped with a certain disorder. One of them, half-nude, plays the role of Bacchus and crowns another with grape leaves. As Ortega y Gasset has astutely observed, Velázquez "throws the gods out [of this canvas] with his brush as if chasing them with a broom. In his Bacchanal not only is there a Bacchus, there is a good-for-nothing who represents Bacchus". Thus "he has prepared the way for our age which is exempt of gods, an administrative age in which instead of Dionysius we speak of alcoholism" (10). X-ray studies have shown an interesting change or two, in the group of drinkers there was one other head. Nevertheless, certain elements of the composition bother us: if the scene were divided on a symmetrical axis we would notice that the majority of the figures occupy the right-hand half.

The First Trip to Italy (1629-1631)

Thanks to the King's aid, Velázquez realizes his desire of visiting Italy. He embarked in Barcelona and made the crossing in the same ship in which Espínola —the victor at Breda who would several years later be immortalized in a famous canvas— was traveling. The route which Velázquez followed through Venice, Ferrara, Bologna, Rome and Naples was fruitful and completed his knowledge of Italian art. To understand to what extent he was susceptible to the influence of that atmosphere we need only contemplate two paintings done in the neighboring country.

The Forge of Vulcan once again introduces mythological themes. But this time with new perspectives. The god, surrounded by the cyclops who help him in his work, receives the visit of Apollo who comes to denounce Venus' adulterous relationship with Mars. The mission is not the noblest and the figure of the wronged husband, Vulcan, poses the problem of Velázquez's humoristic approach to pagan themes. Nevertheless, Professor Angulo rejects this idea, for he sees in Velázquez "an attitude of respect, although it is expressed in the Naturalist style learned in his youth. It is the consequence of his Renaissance intellectual background and his Naturalist artistic background. In contrast to what is always said... he is not echoing the discreditation of the pagan gods, which is so mercilessly demonstrated in our burlesque fables" (11). In any event, it is important to observe that Velázquez only begins the anecdote, without ever handling the scene which follows, when the lovers are discovered in bed and subjected to public shame bound in a net. Does this attitude signify that the painter's purpose is to remain half-way between a serious and a burlesque point of view? He doubtlessly used engravings to compose the picture and he possibly took into account a painting by El Greco (*St. Maurice*); but the most important thing is to see how he broadens the concept of space by separating the figures and makes the air between them be perceived.

Joseph's Tunic presents, on the religious level, similar problems of composition. The personages are distributed harmoniously within a room whose width is emphasized by means of the floor tiles, in a manner similar to that which occurs in Tintoretto's pictures. Nevertheless, in the background a landscape is seen with Titianesque clouds.

The Mature Years in the Court of Philip IV (1631-1648)

An eventful chapter in Velázquez's life opens on his return from Italy. Now he may be considered a mature painter, with a solid prestige at Court which allows him to live outside of the serious ups and downs such as those produced by the fall of the Count-Duke of Olivares in 1643. Our painter must have fulfilled a fundamental role as decorator for the Hall of the Kingdoms in the new Buen Retiro Palace, with an important cycle of pictures. Probably few ensembles in Spanish art have offered a more carefully studied variety of canvases. The most important series has a historical character; the paintings recalled the few happy military moments from Philip IV's reign. Besides, there were portraits and a curious cycle of mythological subjects (the "Labors of Hercules", owed to the brush of Zurbarán) which completed on a symbolic level the exaltation of the monarch called "the Great" due to an irony of history. Velázquez's work in the Hall of the Kingdoms is reflected above all in a masterful canvas which is worthy of a separate analysis.

The Lances or *The Surrender of Breda* (the picture is known by both names) recalls the taking of the Flemish city by Espínola, Marquis of Los Balbases, in 1625. The triumph of the Spanish troops is exalted in a noble and simple manner. The victor cordially receives from the vanquished Justin of Nassau's hands the keys to the city. On the right are the Spaniards with their lances; on the left, the Flemish troops with their pikes. Both groups are formed leaving a space in the center which the two generals occupy. In the background, soldiers and clouds of smoke recall the battle; the city may be partially seen and the clouds which crown the landscape and help to deepen the setting making the horizon visible may also be admired. Thus the artist conceives the peace between the victors and the vanquished with the greatest dignity. And it is not strange that for that reason this painting has ended up becoming sort of a symbol of military virtues. But more exactly it may reveal Velázquez's sensitivity when he interprets a historical theme. Much must be said about the method followed in doing this canvas; this is especially true since we are aided by sketches by the artist himself in which we may see his previous analyses of it. In one may be seen the complete figure of the person who holds the bridle of the horse whose volume occupies the right-hand zone of the picture. In the engravings and paintings of other artists there may be found antecedents which are worth being taken into account. A print of very poor quality by Bernard Salomon, representing Abraham and Melquisedec surely served as a basis for the entire composition. Other canvases, such as one by Rubens of the same biblical theme, one by Veronese, with Christ and the Centurion, one by El Greco of *El Expolio*... may have contributed to the realization of this great canvas (12). Although these may seem like too many precedents, perhaps it would be worth regarding them if we wish understand Velázquez's method of working. The artist did not distinguish himself so much by his use of creative imagination as by his capacity for putting together and masterfully integrating in one picture elements belonging to others.

Within the second Madrilenian period, some religious paintings of high quality should be mentioned. The first (which may be dated in 1631) is full of symbolism; it represents *Christ After the Flagellation* contemplated by the Christian sould and is inspired by a vision of St. Bridget of Sweden. The work (which is exhibited in the National Gallery in London) moves us mostly, as Lafuente Ferrari observed, because of the delicate figure of the soul, protected by an angel; there is a sketch of this preserved (hidden away in the Jovellanos Collection in Gijón) which was itself inspired by something of Dürer's; Justi linked the figure of Christ with Michelangelo's sculpture of St. Maria Sopra Minerva in Rome (13).

Among the most famous of the religious canvases figures the *Christ on the Cross*, in the Prado, in which the figure stands out with supreme dignity against a dark background. It is a shame that a priming coat which is opaque to X-rays keeps us from resolving the doubts as to whether there was at first a landscape there. The picture comes from the San Plácido Convent and various legends have built up around it. It seems that it was donated by Philip IV to the community as proof of repentance for a frustrated amorous adventure which would have had a nun from this house as its victim (14). Above, all, this Christ constitutes a magnificent example of religious exaltation on a strictly human level. Years later, a little after 1640, the *Coronation of the Virgin* must have been painted, full of color and composed with a noble Classicism; the supernatural is strictly reduced to the indispensable; but this note agrees with the artist's taste which tends to unite the earthly and divine elements. A picture by El Greco and an engraving by Dürer on the same topic are alleged as precedents for this canvas.

Another of the great religious paintings which is usually placed in the second Madrilenian period (although due to its style it should be reconsidered as from the last years of the artist's life) is that which represents the *Visit of St. Anthony Abbot to St. Paul the Hermit*. Once more precedents have been pointed out to understand the composition of this painting; Angulo has recalled various engravings by Dürer and a canvas by Patinir among others; nevertheless, it is admirable and full of originality due to its chromatic wealth, the fluid brushwork and the success in contrasting the foreground with the sense of depth developed in the landscape. The open, succulent brush strokes mark this work with an incredible modernity which contrasts with a primitive note: various episodes of the story are represented on the same canvas. St. Anthony, almost transparent, may first be made out in the far background; then his encounter with the centurion is represented; afterwards, with the Satyr; closer, behind the hollowed out rock, he appears calling at the cave where St. Paul lives; in the foreground the two old men finally appear together, while a crow comes down with food in his beak; lastly, in somewhat small dimensions, the story ends with St. Anthony kneeling next to the body of the hermit.

Though the examples discussed up to this point are extraordinarily interesting, it may not be doubted hat Velázquez's principal activity during the second Madrilenian period unfolded in the field of portraits. At the height of his faculties, Velázquez seems to have definitively assimilated everything which his contact with Venetian painters, Rubens and also with El Greco supposed. The series, serving as a transition from the previous period, could be initiated with a female portrait in profile which has been identified as Juana Pacheco, the artist's wife. It stands out against a lighted neutral background which helps to give volume to the face. The personage has a canvas in her hand as if she were a painter or perhaps a *Sibyl*. The mantle adds a note of color which serves as a good introduction to the predominant preoccupations in the portraits from this period.

The decoration of the Hall of the Kingdoms permitted Velázquez to intervene (directly or through his helpers) in the elaboration of portraits of royal personages who are seen in a open-air setting, often times on horseback, standing out against a landscape in the background. Color triumphs and through this these works are contrasted with those of the first Madrilenian period which were set inside rooms and in low light. To understand how the great painter expresses himself in the field of portraits, it may be useful to compare three equestrian ones. That of *Philip IV* in profile (painted thus due to compositional requirements since it flanked a doorway in the Hall of the Kingdoms) with its radiant colors and curious series of "repentances" in the painting of the horse's forelegs also seems to condense in the face all the monarch's weakness if we compare it to the famous portrait of the *Count-Duke of Olivares*. This one shows the horse rearing up facing the background, which acquires a great depth with the presentation of a vast scene flanked by clouds; Olivares appears with all the pomp of a great general and in his arrogant elegance must be seen an act of adulation toward the prime minister who was incapable of directing a battle such as the one which is glimpsed in the far background of the painting. The timid expression of the king and the falsely relaxed one of Don Gaspar de Guzmán contrast with the endearing one of *Prince Baltasar Carlos* which would complete the triptych of equestrian portraits in a canvas in which the ill-fated heir to the throne rides a pony seen in an extremely violent attitude of foreshortening; several engravings have been brought up to justify this perspective; also it has been said that the horse had died and had been stuffed or that since the canvas was conceived to be hung above a doorway it would lose, in place, the effect which it produces when it is seen straight on and not at an angle. In any event, the Prince, painted when he was only five years old, attracts us with the outstanding chromatic qualities of his dress and the delicacy of his expression. The landscape which serves as a background is one of the most lovely ones painted by Velázquez, taking as the setting the Pardo Forest, but adding in the distance the Hoyo and Guadarrama Mountains, which may be identified by the peak of La Maliciosa in the center of the snowy mountains.

The landscape which serves as Madrid's background is also used to provide the setting for other splendid portraits in which the members of the royal family wear hunting costumes. One of the most lovely is that of the *Cardinal-Infante Don Fernando* with his rifle and his dog, standing at ease, silhouetted against a background of clouds. In the same cycle may be included that of *Philip IV* and the one of *Prince Baltasar Carlos*. In these canvases the vision of nature serves to create an atmosphere for some masterfully painted pictures; the dogs represented here reflect Velázquez's extraordinary talent for painting animals, well certified by the *Head of a Deer* which is kept in the Casa Torres Collection.

Very close to the world of royalty are the buffoons, those dwarves and unhappy beings who served as "entertainers" for the Court of Philip IV. In the portraits which Velázquez left us of them there is a great lesson in humanity to be learned. The painter does not concentrate so much on the physical deformitites as on the spiritual qualities. *Don Sebastián de Morra, Don Diego de Acedo "El Primo"*, *"The Boy of Vallecas", Calabacillas, Barbarroja* and *"Don Juan de Austria"* never make us laugh. Rather they cause a profound feeling of affection and friendship in us. Moreno Villa's studies (16) allow us to revive the personalities of these beings in whom human misery on the physical plane can find its counterpoint on the moral level. The chronology of the buffoons is far from being well-established and this is even true for the identity of some of them. It is enough to point out the possibility that in certain cases canvases done in the second Madrilenian period might have been corrected (especially the backgrounds) years later.

Other portraits will place us before personages who were connected with Velázquez and the Court. The likeness which he transmits to us of the great sculptor *Juan Martínez Montañés* is very interesting; it is done at the moment when he is modelling in clay the head which would serve as a model for Pietro Tacca for the famous equestrian statue which is seen in the Oriente Plaza in Madrid. The most illustrious sculptor of religious images in the Sevillian school is conceived here against a neutral background, his head done in light colors standing out against the dark background, while that of the King is sketched in on top of light tones. The face of *Cardinal Borja* remains full of life in a magnificent drawing in the San Fernando Academy and is the starting point for an oil portrait which is known in various versions.

Finally, worth recalling among the portraits of this period are three full-length versions. That of *Pablillos de Valladolid,* the famous actor who could have participated in the festivals organized by the Court in the Buen Retiro, shows the figure with legs spread in a declamatory stance, as if he were performing before the public, and dressed in black; he seems to be floating over the clear space, since in the background nothing is indicated which allows us to find the break between the floor and the walls; the shadow of the legs helps the personage to stand out against this unreal atmosphere. The method would be utilized centuries later by Manet in the *Boy Playing a Flute.* The figures christened *Aesop* and *Mennipus* are somewhat enigmatic. They were painted to decorate the Torre de la Parada in El Pardo. Rather than personages from the

Classical world they show us men from the street captured with a great dignity.

According to what we read in an inscription, in 1647 Juan Bautista Mazo put the finishing touches on a painting which due to its quality must have been begun by his master. It shows a *View of Zaragoza* from the other side of the river, with a series of people skillfully distributed on various planes. As Angulo observes, the figure of the *Man with a Cape* which is seen in a lovely sketch in the San Fernando Academy would not be at odds with this canvas (18).

In 1648, after he has decided upon his second trip to Italy, Velázquez must have passed through *Granada* leaving us a view of the cathedral standing out against the city as a whole, in a delicate drawing in sepia tones. This work is the most interesting one of its genre. Velázquez, with the help of line and shadow, builds the volumes with the same rigor that Cézanne might have used on the threshold of the 20th century.

His Difficult Triumph in Rome (1649-1651)

If the first trip to Italy served to complete Velázquez's education, the second one could reinforce his prestige outside of Spain, after he faced a series of adverse circumstances. For this reason the title which heads this new period is legitimate. He achieves his triumph after he fulfills a thankless task from the King and about which we find disconcerting views. The second trip has its antecedents almost two years before when a series of repairs and alteration is decided upon for the Alcázar which causes Velázquez to act once again as a decorator (after the activities realized in the Buen Retiro) whose importance Justi discovered and Bonet Correa pointed out (19). In brief, we recall that the artist embarks in January of 1649 in Málaga and in the same ships which transported the emissaries charged with receiving Philip IV's new wife, Doña Mariana of Austria. From this it is a far cry to supposing that Velázquez formed part of a diplomatic mission, as Palomino wrote.

Upon arriving in Genoa, our painter would leave the people who made up the mission to head for Venice, going through Milan and Padua. In April he was in the City of the Canals and there he must have begun negotiations leading to the acquisition of art works to decorate the Madrilenian Alcázar. The carrying out of this mission must have filled the artist with displeasure. Some extremely curious letters of Cardinal La Cueva's which the author discovered some years ago prove the fact and they reveal better than any other testimony this bitterness. In one of them he says: "Some guy by the name of Velázquez [note the contemptuous tone], the Valet of the King's Privy Chamber, has come here and says that he has a commission to go around Italy looking at statues and paintings and to try to get the best of them to decorate the Palace in Madrid and... this Court... is... very much against it saying that in these times of such losses and great calamities of all kinds it is not fit to spend time and money on such a frivolous activity, proper to people who don't have anything else to do, look at, or spend money on..." Setting aside other harsh words we remember that in another letter he adds: "The commission to swindle us out of pictures and statues given to the Valet of the King's Privy Chamber Velázquez is spoken of with great shame..." (20). Why should we continue to put down these adverse sentences? The ones above are enough to evoke the criticism of the Roman court in the face of the King of Spain's misgovernment in one of his kingdom's most dramatic moments since Spanish dominion had just been toppled after the serious defeats suffered in the Thirty Years' War.

Velázquez must have had to listen to words as harsh as those of Cardinal La Cueva's but once his mission was completed, we must rejoice in his triumph in Rome which was first exemplified in the fame he achieved after he publicly exhibited, in the Pantheon, a portrait of his servant *Juan de Pareja*. This extremely famous work was acquired in 1970 by the Metropolitan Museum of New York for the highest price ever paid to date for any painting: more than five million dollars! Velázquez was admitted to the San Lucas Academy, named "Fratello" of the "Congregatione dei Virtuosi al Pantheon" and as the culmination of these activities, we would have the works which he does for the Pope, diverse portraits of his family and of the Pontifice himself. The likeness of *Innocent X,* the Dorian Pope, marks the highest level reached by Velázquez in the genre of individual portraits. It is said that the Pope didn't like it too much because the portrait turned out to be "tropo vero", all too life-like, and it is true that nothing more true-to-life may be conceived as far as a psychological assessment of a personage is concerned. For the great painter Reynolds, this painting was the most lovely one which he saw in Rome. It is, needless to say, startling due to the audacity of its coloring: painted in red tones which are used in the arm chair, the clothing, the curtain in the background and even in the flesh, it constitutes a technical ostentation without precedent. Palomino tells us an anecdote which seems to be taken from some writer of Classical antiquity: he says that presence of the canvas fooled one of the Pope's stewards, who when he saw the portrait "thought that it was he in the flesh and went out at once to tell various courtiers who were in the Chamber to lower their voices, because His Holiness was in the next room" (21). The worth of the anecdote should not be exaggerated, because the merits of the work are very far above any possible visual trickery.

During his second stay in Italy Velázquez must have painted the two small pictures which show the *Gardens of the Villa Medici,* although some critics prefer to date them around 1630 and others, due to the diversity of their techniques, favor placing one during each of the two Roman stays (22). It is difficult to make strong statements; in either case the technical elements allow us to emphasize the bravado of the brush strokes and the Impressionist concept which predominates in these landscapes, an anticipation of those which are found in 19th century art. In Spain garden themes interested Velázquez once again. There are various paintings in his style which should be taken into account although they are not of first-rate quality. One of the most representative ones shows The *"Tritons" Fountain in the Gardens of Aranjuez.*

The seated figure of the god *Mars,* which Camón Aznar (23) includes among the buffoons, probably corresponds to this second Italian period. There are some elements in this work, such as the big moustache, which seem to detract from the heroic tone which should be given to the god of war. Doubtlessly, Velázquez wished to interpret it thus not only to leave him without superhuman qualities, but also to strike a pessimistic note which went well with Spain's circumstances. A tired god whose posture at the same time recalls a famous Classical sculpture, the Ludovisi Ares, and another from the Renaissance, the "Pensieroso", by Michelangelo, in the Medici Chapel in Florence.

The cycle of masterpieces from this second Italian period

may be completed with the *Venus at Her Mirror* in the National Gallery in London, which formed part, until the beginning of the 19th century, of the Casa de Alba Coll. Before, this canvas was fixed as one of the last ones by Velázquez; but thanks to a fortunate discovery in the archives of the Casa de Alba (24), we know the work was to be found in the Collection of the Marquis of Heliche (the Count-Duke of Olivares' nephew) in 1651. It is probable that the canvas was painted in Italy if we realize that the representation of female nudes was prohibited for Spanish painters in the 17th century. A series of engravings and even a sculpture reveal the sources which Velázquez used to compose the picture (25); but even so, our esteem for the painting is no less, for it is filled with a chromatic force and is worthy of being counted among the best nudes in the history of painting. Venus is not conceived as a goddess, but as a woman on a realistic plane, which contrasts with the emphasis on fiction in the amorino and the view of her face as reflected in the mirror.

Velázquez's second stay in Italy brings other commentaries to mind even in the light of very recent discoveries. In letters from March and April of 1650 there are negotiations to authorize Velázquez to copy statues in Bellvedere. But for our purpose it is more interesting to recall the impatience of the monarch, who wanted to hasten the artist's return to Spain at any cost. From February of 1650 on, we know of no less than sixteen letters from Philip IV, which must have been pressuring Velázquez. Nevertheless, there is no news of his arrival in Madrid until June 23rd of the following year (26).

His Definitive Conquering of Color and Space (1651-1660)

The last period of Velázquez's life covers a little less than a decade and shows us the painter in very close contact with the Court, fulfilling his obligations as Head Chamberlain of the Palace, busy with the installation of the new rooms in the Alcázar or of other royal lodgings and dedicated to doing paintings of extreme interest.

The mythological themes continue to attract him and in them he attempts to concentrate the fruits of the most diverse and complex experiments. From this point of view, no picture may be compared to *The Weavers*. For a long time it was believed that there was only to be seen in this canvas a scene taken from daily life; in the foreground were seen some women with a distaff, spool and spinning wheel working in the reweaving workshop of the Santa Isabel Tapestry Factory in Madrid; in the background were seen, in a light-filled room, some gentlewomen before some material. But a series of studies done in the last decades have added new importance to the canvas. Now it may be affirmed that the tapestry in the background, in which *The Rape of Europa* is represented (according to a painting by Titian today preserved in Boston) must be connected to the fable, narrated by Ovid, of the contest between Pallas and Arachne. The two personages appear standing, in front of the tapestry. The goddess, shown with a helment, raises her hand to punish the woman from Lydia who tried to prove herself more talented on the loom and had dared to defame Jupiter recalling his amorous adventures in the cloth which she wove. Velázquez chooses the moment inmediately before the metamorphosis of the woman into a spider, being able, thanks to this, to maintain the realistic atmosphere of the whole.

But in *The Weavers* there is not only mythology. Azcárate has recalled the connections which exist between the personages in the foreground and those of an allegorical character which Ripa describes in his "Iconology". Of course, the woman who works on the spinning wheel coincides with an image which must be a symbol of obedience; other symbols may complete the meaning of the picture on a plane which is quite different from that upon which it had traditionally been interpreted. With suprising intuition, Ortega y Gasset thought of the Fates as he observed the work of the weavers; on the other hand, he emphasizes how the painter tries to "keep attention from being fixed on any particular component in the picture and rather make the painting as a whole be what acts on the spectator" (27). In this extremely brief enumeration of iconographic questions, the problems of this exceptional picture are not exhausted. And though the narrative aspect is very useful for understanding Velázquez's intentions, it should not be forgotten that the work is much more important from the strictly pictorial point of view. In the composition, as Angulo observed, he kept very much in mind a fragment from the ceiling of the Sistine Chapel; two of Michelangelo's famous nudes were changed into Weavers. The light and vibrant color exalt the presence of the air within the painting. How far we are from those figures drawn with such great precision corresponding to his Sevillian period! Now the details break down in the face of the energetic brush strokes. Painting must be understood here as a stimulus for our sight, which goes along capturing chromatic sensations, shading, plays of light seen for an instant; everything which, in short, will serve as a starting point for 19th-century Impressionism.

This mythological painting was not the last one done by

Velázquez. Without counting others which must have been lost in the fire in the old Alcázar it is important to mention a canvas which is usually left unnoticed in the Prado Museum and, nevertheless, is masterful: *Mercury and Argos*. The death of Argos, who was surprised by the god while he was sleeping, is conceived within a composition which, once again, might have been based on other works; perhaps an antecedent for the main figure may be seen in the story of Noah as portrayed in the vault of the Sistine Chapel. The play of light helps to outline the two human figures and that of Io in the form of an animal, at rest behind Mercury. Few works permit us, like this one, to feel the direct presence of each color. This painting, conceived along with three others (now lost) to be placed over a doorway, brilliantly closes the cycle of mythological subjects which sets Velázquez completely apart from the painting of his time.

Besides these paintings, during the last decade of his life Velázquez did not interrupt his activity as a portrait artist. We must take into account the canvases which recall personages in the Court. *Queen Doña Mariana of Austria* is shown in a full-length portrait, in silvery tones, like in the lovely Prado version, or in a half-figure, like the "excellent workshop piece" (28) in the San Fernando Academy Museum. *The Infanta María Teresa* (in the Louvre, Vienna and New York) maintains the same stylistic characteristics as her stepmother. Finally, *The Infanta Margarita* may be seen at different ages, from the canvas in the Palacio Liria to the one in the Prado (which remained unfinished), and including the magnificent versions in the Vienna Museum. Along with the feminine portraits, as an exception, there are one or two of the King. The most impressive of all is the one which offers a bust of *Philip IV* with no adornments to distract us; this canvas in the Prado is the most conclusive proof of the painter's dedicated affection for the monarch; it is quite removed from the bearing of a more courtly character in the other works. As Sánchez Cantón has said, here all that we find is "the soul peeking out from the face" (29) of a man who, at the end of his life, has let himself be beaten by his own melancholy.

But of all the works which evoke the Court of Philip IV none is equal to *The Maids of Honor* (*Las Meninas*). The picture of "the family" (it was known by this name until the 18th century) signifies in the field of portraits the decisive formation of ideals which had begun to appear in the Sevillian years. At first glance, the composition seems to be profoundly logical. In the canvas may be seen a room of the old Madrilenian Alcázar in which Velázquez appears, painting a picture, along with a series of other personages. In the center of the scene is the Infanta Margarita who receives a refreshment from one of her maids of honor, Doña Isabel de Velasco; on other side are found Doña Agustina Sarmiento, the dwarf Maribárbola and the dwarf Nicolasillo, who places his foot on the resting dog; in the middleground, a maid of honor, Doña Marcela de Ulloa, turns toward a gentleman who is a ladies' escort; in the background, standing out in an open doorway, we have a personage, Don José Nieto Velázquez, who was also a Palace Chamberlain. Along with these personages whom we see directly, we must remember the bust of Philip IV and Doña Mariana which we may perceive reflected in a mirror. Thanks to this detail, which might seem insignificant, the picture takes on all its meaning. Thus it may be affirmed that what Velázquez must have been painting was a portrait of the royal couple. They were outside of the canvas, in the place where the spectators stand, and thus these latter, by means of this technique, feel a part of this atmosphere as well. The personages in *The Maids of Honor,* therefore, are not looking out at us, but rather toward the king and queen; but the overall effect of unity is achieved in an admirable manner.

With apparently simple methods Velázquez managed to express in *The Maids of Honor* a series of pictorial values which may be discovered after an overall glance at the canvas. The light, as in the case of *The Weavers,* fulfills a decisive role by filtering throught the side windows, by expressing the depth of the setting on beyond Don José Nieto's figure, by "vibrating" in the mirror, by shining directly on the Infanta Margarita. The darling figure of the little girl (who had a sad fate in store, for she died at the age of twenty-two while awaiting the birth of her seventh child) serves as the axis for all the other personages —not only because she occupies the center of the canvas, but because she attracts the spectator's eye thanks to the golden tones and other audacious touches of color used by the artist. When the picture was analyzed with a geometric criterion, it was pointed out that there is a connection between its proportions and those of the Golden Mean. Perhaps it is pure coincidence. But in any event it is undeniable that Velázquez's ideals concerning the representation of figures within a space reach their definitive expression here. Relationships between the atmosphere of this work may be seen with that of other Flemish and Dutch paintings, with antecedents starting from the excellent painting by Jan van Eyck, *The Arnolfini Marriage,* which was in Madrid in Velázquez's time... but no matter what sources inspired the work, it possesses a prodigious originality in its theme, in its composition, in its free and open technique and its fortunate manner in interpreting the effects of the aerial perspective (30).

The date of *The Maids of Honor* (which must have been painted in 1657 or 1658) brings us close to the end of Velázquez's life. Death surprised him as he returned from the French border, where he had been with the King for the occasion of the wedding between Louis XIV and the Infanta María Teresa. Palomino, the best of the artist's biographers, describes his last moments for us: the 31st of July, "he began to feel tired and have sharp pains in his heart; he was constantly thirsty..." Friday, August 6, at two o'clock in the afternoon, "he surrendered his soul to the One who had created him for the world's great admiration, leaving a great impression on all, and not the least on his Majesty, who in the worst moments of his sickness, had let him know how much he cared for him and admired him" (31).

The painter was dressed for burial in the habit of a Knight of the Order of St. James, which he probably wore for the first time, even though in his self-portrait in *The Maids of Honor* he is seen sporting the Apostle's Cross. Almost posthumously he reached the level of dignity which he had probably always desired, making us think of certain aristocratic ambitions which, as is humanly understandable, the artist must have felt. It is not out of place to mention that by a strange twist of fate Velázquez's descendants ended up with the most unforeseeable connections with the royal houses of Europe. A granddaughter of Don Diego's, the daughter of the painter Mazo, was the mother of the Marquis of Monteleón, who married into families of royal descent, among whose descendants we find no less than the Princes of Liechtenstein, the Princess of Luxembourg, Prince Bernard of Holland and Balduino of Belgium (32).

HIS STYLE

The perusal which has just been effected may serve to perceive, besides the trajectory of Velázquez's life, the process of evolution of an art which tends, with a continuous increase in its worth, to enrich painting as a whole with its extremely noble attributes. Beginning in the Sevillian period, under the influence of Tenebrism, with an incisive line, vigorous chiaroscuro and notable lighting effects, Velázquez's style kept on developing from the moment he arrived in Madrid thanks to a growing respect for color. From the earlier harsh realism, achieved with precise lines, we move on to an exaltation of form by means of brush strokes which are richer and richer in their subtleness, in which light continues to play a transcendental role, but filtered through the atmosphere and reflected on every object. The feeling of depth is more intense as the outlines of the objects are "put out of focus" as if atmospheric effects kept us from seeing their lines, or at least blurred them somewhat. Thus, at the height of his faculties, Velázquez interprets reality through a series of appearances which are justified by his vision of "aerial perspectives".

The ultimate understanding of the pictorial values must thus be reached by taking very much into account, as Orozco has done (33), the transcendental role played by color. In many cases the colors are juxtaposed in such a manner that our sight must move from one to another until it reaches the deepest background of the picture, this being emphasized by the lighting effects. And along this road we begin to see a new concept of reality, which is quite removed from what was generally understood as such. Velázquez's reality possesses very peculiar characteristics because it is the fruit of a series of inventions and even tricks which encourage us to penetrate the essence of things. The image which we see reflected in the mirrors of some of his works at times does not coincide with that which would arise on the rigorously physical level, but the results are, nevertheless, much more impressive and obvious.

In this vein, it is worth asking if over and above the strictly pictorial problems we may legitimately discover an intention in Velázquez's work which would show the artist to us as an interpreter of his times. In the measure in which he was a man of his times, of the Baroque period, it is undeniable that his painting contains attributes which are very characteristic of this style of art. When Velázquez's personages in *The Drinkers,* in *The Lances* or in *The Maids of Honor* gaze out from the picture, it seems as if they were trying to meet the spectator's eye, making him a part of his world and aware of his problems. It is possible, therefore, to see in these notes a rupture in the hermetical system which seems to exist in Velázquez's painting in other cases. It is not far-fetched to venture that his Baroque outlook is in line with the fluctuating trajectory of the same which, on a literary plane, runs from Cervantes to Calderón.

Following this path, may we find in Velázquez's paintings a criticism of the society of his times? Maravall saw in the portraits the best expression of an epoch, that of Descartes; thus they may be converted into a basis for understanding the first steps toward the modern world (34). It is difficult to set the limits of this doctrine. Although the critical intent of Velázquez's painting may not be extreme, it is still worthy of interest as documentation for an epoch, especially the period which was his to live in Spain: that of Philip IV. The lack of joy, the melancholy of Velázquez's personages may serve to sum up an unfortunate period of our political history which paradoxically was a golden time in the field of arts and letters (35).

NOTES

1. **Tres horas en el Museo del Prado.** Madrid, Aguilar, 12th ed., 1957. (The same publisher has issued an English-language edition, **Three hours in the Prado Museum.** Translator's note.)

2. Ortega's interest in Velázquez is significant because the great thinker never commented so repeatedly on any other artist; Gaya Nuño's **Bibliografía** lists 13 entries (Nos. 1253 to 1265), although some of them refer to various editions of the same work. The most complete analysis of these works is by Lafuente Ferrari (**Velázquez en Ortega y Gasset.** «Varia Velazqueña», pp. 579-612).

3. Of the three works cited by Gaya Nuño (Nos. 1034-1036) the most important is the book **Velázquez y el espíritu de la modernidad,** in which the artist appears as an interpreter of the ideas that gave birth to the modern world.

4. In **«Las Meninas, fantasía Velazqueña en dos actos»,** premiered December 9, 1960, the author makes a free interpretation of a Velázquez confronted by the Inquisition for having painted the **Venus at her Mirror;** in spite of some inaccuracies, several figures are very well characterized.

5. See the **Homenaje poético a Velázquez** that appears in **Goya** (Nos. 37-38, 1960) and other texts listed by Gaya Nuño.

6. Readers interested in the problems of the evaluation of the paintings of Velázquez should refer to López Rey's catalogue, which is mentioned in the Bibliography. The versions registered for many paintings give one an idea of the significance of the copies or other works produced in the painter's workshop alongside the strictly original ones.

7. In **Arte de la pintura, su antigüedad y sus grandezas** (Seville, 1649; there are other editions, from 1866 and 1946), Pacheco has left us this and other important texts about Velázquez which are invaluable for understanding his formation.

8. **Op. cit.**

9. See page 212 of **Velázquez** in the Austral Collection (2nd edition, 1970) which brings together several of Ortega's texts about the artist.

10. In the interesting article, **Tres cuadros del vino,** published in «El Espectador» and reprinted in «Notas» (see Vol. 45 of the Austral Collection), where a comparison is made of the «bacchanals» of Titian, Poussin and Velázquez. With regard to **The Drinkers,** see also the texts of Carducho, Cruzada Villamil, Soria, Borelius and Angulo which Gaya Nuño cites in his **Bibliografía.**

11. **Velázquez y la Mitología.** Madrid, Instituto de España, 1961. See also the other works on the subject by the same author in «Archivo Español de Arte» and «Goya» (1960). Also of interest are the articles by Colombier and Soria in Gaya Nuño's **Bibliografía.**

12. The comentaries on this painting are numerous. The Marquis of Lozoya has written a monograph; but there are also interesting contributions by Angulo (**Velázquez. Cómo compuso sus principales cuadros**), Sánchez Cantón, Borelius and Soria, listed in Gaya Nuño's bibliography.

13. The head of Christ may be related to the drawing in the National Library of Madrid (No. 496 in Barcia's catalogue).

14. Recommended to the reader is the work by Marañón, **Don Juan** (Madrid, Collection Austral, No. 129), in which allusion is made to this and other stories of the Madrilenian convent.

15. See Angulo: **Velázquez. Cómo compuso sus principales cuadros...**

16. **Locos, enanos, negros y niños palaciegos. Gente de placer que tuvieron los Austrias en la Corte española desde 1663 a 1770.** México, Casa Española en México, 1939.

17. See Pérez Sánchez, Alfonso E.: **Catálogo de los Dibujos.** Real Academia de San Fernando. Madrid, 1967. Page 152.

18. **Cuarenta dibujos españoles.** Dibujos de la Real Academia de San Fernando. Madrid, 1966. Page 36. A document kept in the Palacio de Liria shows that a version of the **View of Zaragoza** had an allegory of the Virgin of the Pillar in the upper half. Velázquez may have followed El Greco's idea in the latter's **View of Toledo.** See José Manuel Pita Andrade: **Noticias en torno a Velázquez en el Archivo de la Casa de Alba.** «Varia Velazqueña», p. 400.

19. **Velázquez arquitecto y decorador.** «Archivo Español de Arte», 1960, pp. 215-249.

20. See the author's article: **Noticias en torno a Velázquez...**, cited in Note 18.

21. The biography of Velázquez that appears in **Museo Pictórico y Escala Optica** by the painter Acisclo Antonio Palomino de Castro (Madrid, 1724) is the most important of all as a work done with the aid of numerous contemporary documents. Of interest are not only anecdotes such as this, but also other testimonies which contribute to making a profile of the artist's human personality.

22. In the most recent studies such as the ones by López Rey and Camón Aznar, the date 1630 is once again preferred, deriving support from the fact that Velázquez lived in the Villa Medici during his first trip. Orozco and Bonet prefer to date them apart. Here, for stylistic reasons, we shall maintain that the second date is correct for both.

23. **Velázquez.** Madrid, Espasa Calpe, 1964.

24. Pita Andrade, José Manuel: **Los cuadros de Velázquez y Mazo que poseyó el séptimo Marqués del Carpio.** «Archivo Español de Arte», 1952, pp. 223-236.

25. The works on the **Venus at her Mirror** are numerous. Until 1943 the most complete bibliography was Neil MacLaren's **The Rokeby Venus** (London «The Gallery Books», No. 1); afterwards, one must see, among others, the commentaries that appear in «Varia Velazqueña», «Archivo Español de Arte» and «Goya» with regard to 1960 and the tercentenary of the artist. Above all, see the study by Sánchez Cantón.

26. A summary of the artist's journey is to be found in the author's article, **El itinerario de Velázquez en su segundo viaje a Italia,** «Goya», 1960, p. 151. The most recent work with new documentary data is the one by Domingo Martínez de la Peña y González: **El segundo viaje de**

Velázquez a Italia: **dos cartas inéditas en los archivos del Vaticano.** «Archivo Español de Arte», No. 173, 1971, pp. 1-7.

27. More commentaries have been written about this and **Las Meninas** than any other painting by Velázquez. The reader may refer to Gaya Nuño's bibliography and see the works cited by Angulo, María Luisa Caturla, Azcárate, De Tolnay, Laín and Ortega, with some paragraphs of a letter to Paulino Garagorri, who also published an article about this painting.

28. Fernando Labrada: **Catálogo de pinturas.** Real Academia de San Fernando. Madrid, 1965, No. 633.

29. **Los retratos de los Reyes de España.** Barcelona, Ed. Omega, 1948.

30. As in the case of **The Weavers,** there are many commentaries on this work. It has been studied monographically by Sánchez Cantón in **Velázquez. Las Meninas y sus personajes.** Barcelona, Ed. Juventud, 1943. Included in this excellent work is a bibliography up to that date. Later, there have appeared commentaries by the Marqués de Saltillo, Emmens, Leiris, Ramiro Moya, De Tolnay, Alpatov, Angulo, Cirici Pellicer, Paul Claudel and Díaz Plaja which where compiled in Gaya Nuño's bibliography. Afterwards, one must recall, among other analyses, those by Camón Aznar and the article by Jesús María Caamaño in the «Revista de Ideas Estéticas» (1970) in which the ties with Van Eyck's portrait of Giovanni Arnolfini and his wife are insisted upon. In another sphere, we should recall to the imprint left by this canvas on later painting and especially on Picasso, who painted his famous versions of **Las Meninas** exactly three hundred years after they had been created by Velázquez.

31. Besides the testimony of Palomino, which appears in the work cited in note 21, see the article by Laín Entralgo, **La muerte de Velázquez,** in «Archivo Español de Arte», 1960, pp. 101-107.

32. About the «aristocratic pruriences», see López Rey: **Nombres y nombradía de Velázquez.** «Goya», Nos. 37-38, 1960, pp. 4-5. Regarding his unusual descendants, see Alberto de Mestas: **Descendencia regia de un pintor de reyes,** «Hidalguía», VIII, No. 42, 1960, pp. 661-688.

33. Emilio Orozco Díaz: **La función compositiva del color en la pintura de Velázquez.** «Revista de Ideas Estéticas», 1961. This work was printed with others that contribute to an evaluation of the painter's style in a volume entitled **El barroquismo de Velázquez.** Madrid, Ediciones Rialp, 1965.

34. See the work cited in note 3.

35. Limitations of space do not allow further treatment Velázquez' style. There are many facets. To be recommended are the works cited in Gaya Nuño's bibliography, by the author himself, by Lafuente Ferrari, Julián Gállego, Moreno Villa, Chueca Goitia, Camón Aznar, etc.

BIBLIOGRAPHY

There are many important studies of Velázquez. The ones published up to 1963 were brought together in a fundamental work by Juan Antonio GAYA NUÑO: *Bibliografía crítica y antológica de Velazquez* (Madrid, Fundación Lázaro Galdiano). In this volume commentaries are made on 1814 works, along with a broad introduction in which the most important contributions are evaluated in chronological order. Among the monographs which must be singled out, in order of appearance, are those written by Cruzada Villamil, Curtis, Beruete, Justi, Mayer, Moreno Villa, Lafuente, Trapier, Pantorba and Ortega. After the publication of Gaya Nuño's *Bibliografía* came the works of LÓPEZ REY, José: *Velázquez, A Catalogue Raisonné of his Oeuvre, with an Introductory Study*. London, Faber and Faber, 1963; and *Velázquez, His Work and World*. London, Faber and Faber, 1968. In Spain, the most important single contribution has been made by CAMÓN AZNAR, José: *Velázquez*. Madrid, Espasa Calpe, 1964. 2 vols., with numerous illustrations and acute commentaries on the artist's work. A very useful synthesis, with a direct analysis of Velázquez' work made by genre is Juan José MARTÍN GONZÁLEZ: *Velázquez*. Monografía de Arte. Bilbao, Ed. Moretón, 1968.

Texts and documents relating to Velázquez up to the 19th century have been collected in the work directed by Antonio GALLEGO BURÍN and published by the Dirección General de Bellas Artes, to commemorate the artist's tercentenary: *Varia Velazqueña*. Madrid, 1960. 2 vols.

In the notes to the text reference is made in each case to certain works which are of interest for enlarging upon the content of the same.

BLACK AND WHITE PHOTOGRAPHS

PLATE 1. SUPPOSED SELF-PORTRAIT.—Prado Museum.—Oil on canvas. 0.53×0.39 m. The only absolutely unquestionable self-portrait of Velázquez is the one that appears in *Las Meninas*. Among the most likely is this one, which may be dated around 1623.

PLATE 2. HEAD OF A WOMAN.—National Library, Madrid.— Drawing in black pencil on paper. 150×177 mm. A half-profile, the first of two versions kept in the National Library in Madrid. Of great quality, both drawings are usually dated around 1618, and are considered to be portraits of Juana Pacheco.

PLATE 3. SUPPOSED PORTRAIT OF JUANA PACHECO OR SYBIL.—Prado Museum.— Oil on canvas. 0.62×0.50 m. Undated canvas possibly painted around 1632. There is something enigmatic about this nearly half-length figure in profile.

PLATE 4. SOR JERONIMA DE LA FUENTE.—Prado Museum.— Oil on canvas. 1.60×1.10 m. The canvas is signed «Diego Velázquez F. 1620». It comes from the Franciscan Convent of Santa Isabel in Toledo; it was acquired by the Museum in 1944. A copy is kept in the Araoz Collection.

PLATE 5. DON DIEGO DEL CORRAL Y ARELLANO.—Prado Museum.— Oil on canvas. 2.15×1.10 m. Undated but probably just prior to the death of the subject, a lawyer and a knight of the Order of Santiago, in 1632.

PLATE 6. THE SCULPTOR JUAN MARTINEZ MONTAÑES.— Prado Museum.—Oil on canvas. 1.09×1.07 m. It is supposed that the portrait of the famous image-carver (d. 1638), was painted during a trip he made to Madrid two years earlier.

PLATE 7. PABLO DE VALLADOLID.—Prado Museum.—Oil on canvas. 2.08×1.23 m. The subject, commonly called *Pablillos*, was brought to the royal court to act in comedies in 1632, so that the painting may be considered to be from that period. The figure seems to float in space.

PLATE 8. THE BUFFOON «DON JUAN DE AUSTRIA.—Prado Museum,—Oil on canvas. 2.10×1.23 m. The date of this painting is unknown, although it is considered by some as belonging to the second Madrid period (c. 1636) and by others, to the last period. The subject, whose real name is not known, is seen in a room and through the opening behind him on the right there is a kind of naval battle, probably an allusion to the Battle of Lepanto. This refers to the nickname of the buffoon, who also has pieces of armor at his feet which may in turn refer to that used by the illegitimate son of Charles V.

PLATE 9. CRISTOBAL DE CASTAÑEDA, PERNIA, «BARBARRO-JA».—Prado Museum.—Oil on convas. 1.98×1.21 m. Undated painting which can be documented through its style as between 1637 and 1640. The half-length figure is rich in color and is distinguished by a certain monumental presence.

PLATE 10. AESOP.—Prado Museum.—Oil on canvas. 1.78×0.94 m. The name appearing in the upper right-hand corner of the canvas justifies the title of the painting.

PLATE 11. DON DIEGO DE ACEDO, «EL PRIMO».—Prado Museum.—Oil on canvas. 1.07×0.82 m. Believed painted in Fraga in 1644, with the masterly portrait of Philip IV (Frick Coll., N.Y.). The identification of the subject presents the problem indicated in the commentary on Plate XXI.

PLATE 12. CARDINAL BORJA.—Museum of the Academy of San Fernando, Madrid.—Drawing in black pencil. 190×120 mm. A work of exceptional quality. Framed in an oval as if it were being prepared for an engraving which we do not know of. The subject was born in 1582 and was the Duke of Gandía's son. A cardinal since 1611, he was named Archbishop of Toledo in 1643. The drawing may have been done after the latter date.

PLATE 13. MAN WITH A CLOAK.—Museum of the Academy of San Fernando, Madrid.—Drawing in black pencil. 392×226 mm. A work of great quality, even though opinions vary as to whether it should be attributed to Velázquez. It may be a preparatory study for a painting with several figures such as the ones that appear in the *View of Zaragoza*, of 1648.

PLATE 14. VIEW OF GRANADA WITH THE CATHEDRAL.—National Library, Madrid.—Ink and sepia wash drawing. 183×308 mm. Generally unquestioned as to its authenticity, is must have been drawn in 1648 when the artist went through Granada. The vantage point is the subject of discussion; Gómez Moreno thinks it a house near the Church of San José where Alonso Cano may have lived; Lafuente, on the hill of the Alhambra itself; Gallego y Burín, the house of the Admiral of Aragon.

PLATE 15. THE «TRITONS» FOUNTAIN IN THE GARDENS OF ARANJUEZ.—Prado Museum.— Oil on canvas. 2.48×2.23 m. A work which is quite representative of the projection of Velázquez' art into landscape painting. The hand of his pupils can be detected in the general handling. The quality of the composition of the fountain among the great trees and with figures in the foreground is undeniable. There is an inscription which reads: «By order of his Majesty. In the Year 1657».

PLATE 16. THE GOD MARS.—Prado Museum.—Oil on canvas. 1.79×0.45 m. An important, if undated, work. Perhaps painted during Velázquez' second trip to Italy. The reflective, melancholy attitude recalls Michelangelo's statue of Lorenzo de Medici; the composition might be related to the *Ludovisi Ares*.

COLOR PLATES

PLATE I. THE ADORATION OF THE MAGI.—Prado Museum.—
Oil on canvas. 2.03×1.25 m. Painted when the artist was eighteen to twenty years old, depending on how one reads the date,
«1617» or «1619», in the lower part. A masterpiece of the Seville
period, it reflects astonishing sureness in the drawing and composition, attaining an accentuated naturalism in the figures. The
light is concentrated on the Virgin and on the Child, who is
dressed according to Pacheco's suggestions and in conflict with
the styles of the Renaissance. The outdoor scene has been
adapted to the criteria of Caravaggism.

PLATE II. THE INFANTE DON CARLOS.— Prado Museum.—
Oil on canvas. 2.09×1.25 m. Undated; it has been placed between
1623 and 1628. Stylistically it could be equidistant between the
Seville period and the first trip to Italy. The full-length figure,
with legs apart, stands out against a dark background which is
barely modelled by a few shadows. The canvas has been wide-
ned with strips of cloth on either side. The subject, Philip IV's
brother, was born in 1607 and died in 1632.

PLATE III. PHILIP IV AS A YOUNG MAN.—Prado Museum.—
Oil on canvas. 2.01×1.02 m. Undated; from the first Madrid
period, it should be compared with the preceding one. The va-
riations are summarized in the more luminous background, in
the presence of a table with a hat on it and in the change of
posture. The legs are closer together due to retouching; the cape
has been corrected; and the left hand must rest on the pommel
of the sword and not (contrary to what is generally said) on the
table, which is behind him. The portrait of Don Carlos probably
preceded this one by about two years. Both figures, as Camón
Aznar has pointed out, appear remote from the spectator.

PLATES IV - VI. THE DRINKERS.—Prado Museum.—Oil on
canvas. 1.65×2.25 m. A payment of one hundred ducats for «a
picture of Bacchus which was done as a service to his Majesty»
was documented on the 22nd of July, 1629. It is the first to
deal with a mythological subject and contrasts the reality of a
group of «tavern roisterers» (as Ortega y Gasset called them)
with that of the half-nude god of wine who is crowning one of
the drinkers with vine branches. Also for the first time we see
one of Velázquez' backgrounds with oak forests, behind the
grapevines of the foreground.

PLATE VII. HEAD OF A WOMAN.— Lázaro Galdiano Museum.
Madrid.—Oil on canvas. 0.25×0.18 m. Is this exquisite little
painting the «Head of a Galician Woman» cited in the inventory
of pictures belonging to the seventh Marquis del Carpio, nephew
and heir to the Count-Duke of Olivares, as Buendía supposes?
(*Goya*, No. 23, 1958, p. 281). The measurements almost concur.

On comparing this face with others of the Seville period, it is possible to think of a woman who posed for the painter several times. Is she Juana Pacheco? Worth pointing out are the qualities of the head, outlined against a dark background, which acquires a liveliness thanks to the reddish touches in the lips, cheeks, ear and in the ribbon that holds back the hair.

PLATES VIII - IX. THE FORGE OF VULCAN.—Prado Museum.— Oil on canvas. 2.23×2.90 m. Painted during Velázquez' first trip to Italy, around 1630, it alludes to the visit which Apollo made to Vulcan to disclose Venus' adultery with Mars. The god of fire, converted into a symbol of the cuckolded husband, and the Cyclops express their surprise. The dynamic postures of these personages reflect a great interest in the human figure. The painter is at once concerned with the effects of light (much less contrasted and better distributed than in earlier periods) and with the evaluation of things themselves.

PLATES X - XI. CHRIST ON THE CROSS.—Prado Museum.— Oil on canvas. 2.48×1.69 m. Undated, it must be placed within the first five years of the second Madrid period. With four nails, its composition reminds us of the image by Martínez Montañés in the Cathedral of Seville, although in the sculpture the legs are crossed. Few works exalt the human figure, the idea of God made Man, with greater emotion and sobriety. The flesh-tones show the great wealth of nuances in the brushstrokes, testifying to advances in technique in relation to the works of the Seville period.

PLATES XII - XVI. THE LANCES (SURRENDER OF BREDA).— Prado Museum.— Oil on canvas. 3.07×3.67 m. Painted around 1635 for the Hall of the Kingdoms in the Buen Retiro Palace of Madrid. It recalls the surrender of Breda to Spanish troops in 1625 and represents the moment in which Justin of Nassau handed over to keys of the city to Ambrogio Spínola. The composition is based on engravings and several paintings which are of interest, less for what they reveal of sources of inspiration than for showing the path Velázquez followed in creating one of the masterpieces of universal painting.

PLATE XVII. THE COUNT-DUKE OF OLIVARES ON HORSE-BACK.—Prado Museum.—Oil on canvas. 3.23×2.37 m. The latest date for this painting has been established by the protection offered Velázquez by Olivares in 1643; but it may date from up to ten years earlier. Despite its adulatory tone, this is the greatest of all of the portraits of the Count-Duke. The study of the rearing horse and movement of the figure are admirable. The landscape is important as a frame for the equestrian portrait.

PLATES XVIII - XIX. PRINCE BALTASAR CARLOS ON HORSE-BACK.—Prado Museum.—Oil on canvas. 2.09×1.73 m. It may be dated around 1635. It was painted for a cornice in the Hall of the Kingdoms in the Buen Retiro Palace. Of all the portraits of the Prince, this one shows the greatest wealth of color in the figure, with a beautiful landscape of the Sierra de Guadarrama background. Born in 1629 and died in 1646, he would have been six years old, then, when this painting was done.

PLATE XX. PRINCE BALTASAR CARLOS AS A HUNTER.— Prado Museum.—Oil on canvas. 1.91×1.03 m. Contemporary of the preceding painting since at the bottom of it one reads «ANNO AETATIS SUAE VI». The figure of the prince stands in the foreground. He carries a rifle and is flanked by two dogs (one of them is almost not visible because the canvas had to be cut); further back, a tree frames the figure; in the background is the Sierra de Guadarrama. The work is filled with serene placidity.

PLATE XXI. DON SEBASTIAN DE MORRA.—Prado Museum.— Oil on canvas. 1.06×0.81 m. The chronology of this and other Velázquez buffoons presents a serious problem made worse by the matter of identification. This one died in 1649, but in an inventory of the Casa de Alba Archives «a portrait of «El Primo», seated on the ground, with a Walloon hat, dressed in black with a red overcoat trimmed in gold, original by Belazquez» is mentioned (see Pita: *Noticias en torno a Velázquez...*, page 410). In view of this data, should the traditional attributions be varied? Is this figure really Don Diego de Acedo, called «El Primo»? Apart from this we should point out the quality and gravity of the portrait, which causes us to think, not of a grotesque being, but rather of one filled with spirit.

PLATE XXII. CALABACILLAS.—Prado Museum.—Oil on canvas. 1.06×0.83 m. Also called *«The Half-wit of Coria».* This personage died in 1639, thus the latest possible date for the canvas. His name, Juan Calabazas (literally John Gourds), is reflected in the gourds in the picture. The painting shows corrections which may have been made after the death of the subject himself.

PLATE XXIII. THE BOY OF VALLECAS.—Prado Museum.— Oil on canvas. 1.07×0.83 m. This buffoon was also called *Francisco Lezcano* and had the nickname of *El Vizcaino.* He died in 1649. The figure stands out against a dark background, but on the right one sees a landscape which contributes to the effects of light and space.

PLATE XXIV. GARDENS OF THE VILLA MEDICI IN ROME.— Prado Museum.—Oil on canvas. 0.48×0.42 m. The lighter colors of the portico closed with thick boards contrast with the vibrant greens of the box-wood and the cypress trees that crown the painting with vertical elements. Lafuente has observed how «the classical, even academic, appearance of the architecture is counterbalanced by details which, without deforming the composition, seem to leave in its noble lines the negligent and inevitable stamp of life».

PLATE XXV. GARDENS OF THE VILLA MEDICI IN ROME.—
Prado Museum.—Oil on canvas. 0.44×0.38 m. The composition
of the painting is governed by three planes. In the foreground,
two figures and a tree the foliage of which barely hides the
portico that lies on a second plane; under the central arch, the
figure of Ariadne. In the background, some houses are hinted
at, and above them, the vertical lines of the cypress trees. The
comparison of this canvas (with its almost transparent brushstrokes) and the preceding one explains the variety of criteria
concerning the chronology of the two landscapes, as we have
pointed out in the text.

PLATES XXVI - XXVII. THE WEAVERS.—Prado Museum.—Oil
on canvas. 2.20×2.87 m. This is the most complex of Velázquez'
mythological paintings. It represents *The Fable of Arachne*, but
surely contains other allegories as well. The composition is
derived from a fragment of the Michelangelo frescoes on the
ceiling of the Sistine Chapel. Its greatest interest stems, however,
from the pictorial qualities, in the masterly handling of light
and in the unity of concept which dominates the work.

PLATE XXVIII. QUEEN MARIANA.—Museum of the Academy
of San Fernando, Madrid.—Oil on canvas. 0.66×0.40 m. The
second wife of Philip IV is represented «...half-length, with a
head-dress of black silk, white feathers and adornments of
pearls». (Labrada: *Catálogo de las pinturas...* No. 633). Even
though this work is considered to be from the painter's workshop, it was dated by Allende Salazar between 1652 and 1653. It
is among the best canvases done by Velázquez' pupils, although
the master himself probably supervised its creation.

PLATES XXIX - XXXI. THE MAIDS OF HONOR («LAS ME-
NINAS»).—Prado Museum.—Oil on canvas. 3.18×2.76 m. Dated
between 1657 and 1658. In Velázquez' time it was known by the
name of *The Family* and this really seems the most appropriate
in view of the atmosphere of home-like intimacy that prevails
here. The present name appeared in the 18th century. A masterpiece of universal painting, is synthesizes all of the artist's
experiences in his eagerness to bring to the canvas the sensation
of space filtered by light and with full use of color.

PLATE XXXII. THE INFANTA MARGARITA.—Prado Museum.—
Oil on canvas. 2.12×1.43 m. It may be considered Velázquez'
last work, since it was found, unfinished, in his workshop when
he died. The last brushstrokes may have been made by his pupil
and son-in-law, Mazo. Nevertheless, it is a masterpiece for the
rendering of the cloth, and especially for the freedom of the
silvery tones. The Infanta, who presides over *Las Meninas*, was
painted again and again by Velázquez and like so many of
Philip IV's children, she died prematurely, before reaching the
age of twenty-two, while expecting her seventh child.

PLATE 1

PLATE 2

PLATE 3

PLATE 4

PLATE 5

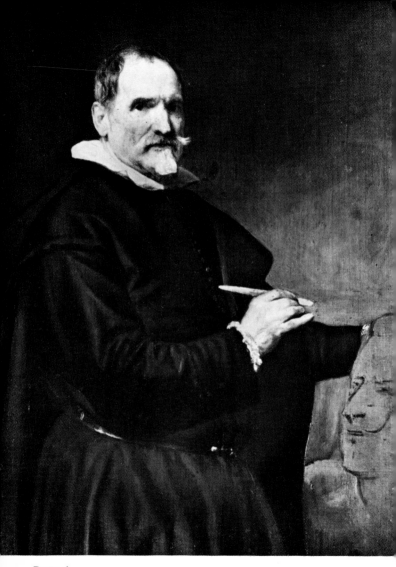

PLATE 6

PLATE 7

PLATE 8

PLATE 9

ÆSOPVS

PLATE 10

PLATE 11

PLATE 12

PLATE 13

PLATE 14

PLATE 15

Plate 16

PLATE I

PLATE II

PLATE III

PLATE IV

PLATE V

PLATE VI

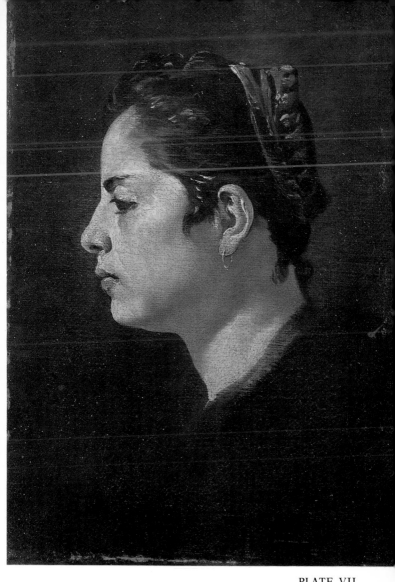

PLATE VII

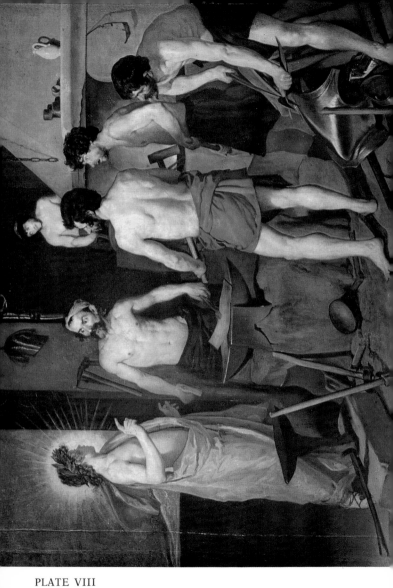

PLATE VIII

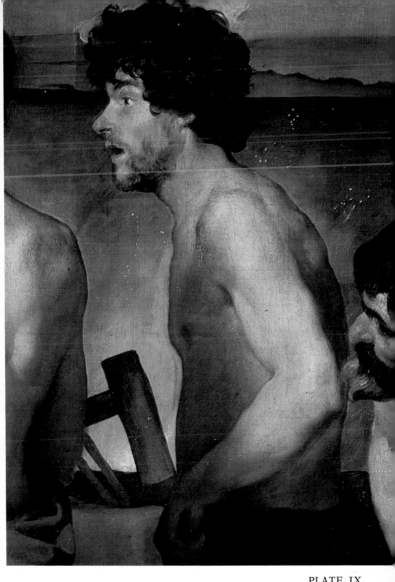

PLATE IX

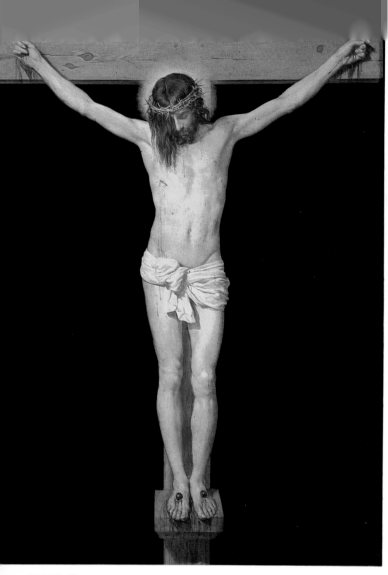

PLATE X

PLATE XI

PLATE XII

PLATE XIII

PLATES XIV and XV

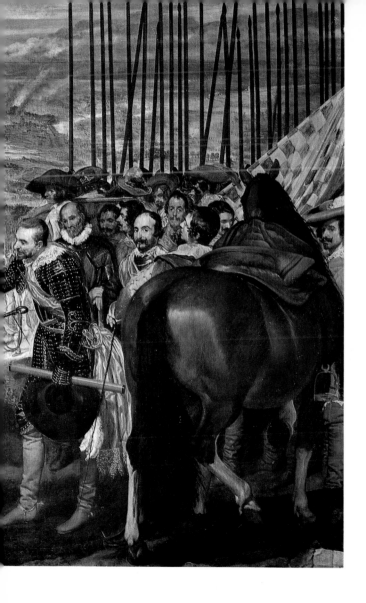

PLATE XVI

PLATE XVII

PLATE XVIII

PLATE XIX

PLATE XX

PLATE XXI

PLATE XXII

PLATE XXIII

PLATE XXIV

PLATE XXV

PLATE XXVI

PLATE XXVII

PLATE XXVIII

PLATE XXIX

PLATE XXXII